The Curse
of the
Sea Witch

Books by the same author:

2 Steps Behind

A Bear called Basher

The Princess & the Chimney Sweep

Magnus, Aye-Aye and the Flying Saucer

Running with Wolves

The Boy from the Saltmarsh

The Elephants' Mirror

Burnt Toast

Another Place Another Time

The Curse

of the

Sea Witch

Dawn Lawrence

Published by
Aldabra Publishing
'Five Wishes' Jarvis Close
Stalbridge, Dorset
DT10 2PQ

Text Dawn Lawrence 2020

First Published 2020
by Aldabra Publishing
'Five Wishes', Stalbridge, Dorset DT10 2PQ

Copyright Dawn Lawrence 2020

Printed in Great Britain by

Unit 4, Barton View business Park, Sheeplands Lane
Sherborne Dorset
DT9 4FW

ISBN 978-1-9162035-3-2

To a bevy of girls:

Maelona, Bethan, Etholle, Jessica, Hannah,
Katie, Emily, Ella, Alys, Elliana

Once a boy but now no more
He lingers still by sea and shore,
His form, his voice, no longer heard
Now charms as some wild beast or bird;
He comes as dawn breaks from the deep
When slipping from the edge of sleep;
Carried on the wind his calls
Across the water still enthrals
Of reed pipe, bird, we know not which,
From kingdoms of the wild Sea Witch;
His form lives on – a mystery
To those who loved him such as we;
The sea has taken him and yet
His spirit haunts lest we forget.

The Curse of the Sea Witch

1

Carys was practising what she liked to call 'magic.' She was always doing things like that – thinking of new ideas and landing herself in situations from which she couldn't escape. Recipes for disaster her friends called it. But then she met someone who could *really* do magic – the kind she dreamed of.

For some particular reason on this particular day as she sat trying to concentrate on a new spell she had devised, her attention was drawn to that occasion. It was OK now to smile at the recollection but it was far from fun at the time.

Her idea had been a magical cure for all ills made entirely from herbs. Having successfully tried it out on herself and a few friends in the group she travelled with, she had grown confident enough to sell some of the potions in local villages. All seemed to go well for a while, but then a lot of people complained of stomach upsets and blamed her. The word 'poison' was even mentioned she recalled. No good trying to explain that it was a virus going around. No, it was her fault, and just to prove their small mindedness she had been kept a prisoner in an old deserted mill until the villagers decided what to do with her. Talk about taking the law into one's own hands!

But she had one staunch friend and helper she could always depend on - her friend Jac - a crow she had rescued as a fledgling. She had taught him to carry messages tied to his leg, and this worked well. Her SOS was picked up by a brother and sister, Morgan and Kyle, living out on the marshes with a mysterious boy, Finn. They had followed Jac to the mill where she was imprisoned and rescued her. It was then that she learnt of the amazing shape-shifting abilities of which Finn was a master. He came to her rescue yet again when she had a near death experience on the marshes trying to locate the place where he lived.

The girl, Morgan, was named after the wicked young witch who beguiled the wizard Merlin in his old age. Morgan kept notes of the time she and her brother lived with Finn. It was a kind of diary of those times when Finn made the impossible become possible.

But then one day he just disappeared … walked into the sea and never came back. Morgan and Kyle managed to get in touch and tell what happened; how they often spoke about him and asked endless questions to which there were no answers.

Carys was sad but she didn't believe Finn had drowned. She often pictured him in dreams when she couldn't sleep, travelling through endless oceans and strange worlds to find that other half of himself which once lived on the land.

She sighed. Life was becoming more and more difficult. She peered over at the book where she had written down the spell she was working on. Just as she did so, the door behind her opened, and a grinning face emerged. It was Ben, one of the travellers who shared their old camper. In his hand he held her morning cup of coffee.

'Hey, Carys, you're not still working on that conundrum of yours! We thought you'd discovered a doorway to another world by now.'

Turning to face him, she grinned back. She was used to lots of teasing.

'C'mon, get a move on. We're sitting out on the rocky part of the beach today. Lovely and warm out there.'

Muttering her thanks, she took the coffee, and the door closed. Standing up, she caught a glimpse of herself in the mirror opposite.

"Just a slip of a girl" Finn had called her. And she was certainly that; her thin, hollow-cheeked features and lank mousy hair not adding anything favourable to her appearance. It was one of the reasons she had decided to immerse herself in magic following in the footsteps of her grandmother who had dabbled a lot in the subject. But only her very few friends were aware of her addiction; to everyone else it was something she kept quiet about, especially since she was such a novice.

Having finished her coffee, she decided to take Ben's advice and join the others outside.

They had found the site by accident, a wildlife area on the coast which was exactly to their liking. The group were gathered beneath the brow of rugged cliffs dropping down sharply to the sea.

'You should have brought your coffee out here,' Ben called as soon as she appeared.

'Yes, you don't get enough sunshine stuck in a dark corner all the time,' Izzy added, as she applied generous amounts of sun lotion to her arms and legs. Isabel - Izzy for short - was the only other girl. And she was everything that Carys was not, being a tall curvy blonde. There was not much to choose between the brothers, Ben and Josh; both being rather on the plump side, both wearing identical T shirts and grubby jeans.

Carys sat down on one of the rugs spread between some rocks, and waited for the questions she knew would come.

'Well—and how did the spell go? Have you learnt it off by heart yet?' Josh grinned at her irritatingly.

'Well, almost,' Carys replied, trying not to lose her temper. 'It's simple really.'

'I don't believe you,' he replied. 'If it's so simple, show us.'

'You don't believe me?' Carys felt her face getting redder and more flushed by the moment, and it had nothing to do with the sun. 'Very well, I'll show you,' she said, knowing full well that she would regret her words later.

'And how do you propose to do that?' Ben laughed, giving his brother a wink.

'The very first person who comes along the beach I'll change into a—a tiger! And I hope it eats you!'

Izzy gave a little scream of laughter and put her sun lotion to one side. This was going to be interesting.

'I like it when you lose your temper,' Josh taunted.

Carys glared at him.

'Look!' Izzy cried, pointing. 'There's someone coming now. You'd better get your act together quickly.'

Everyone looked up. They could just see a figure in the distance, too far away to be recognizable, and without pausing to think

Carys stretched out one hand and uttered a string of words. A second later there was a kind of flash, and the figure disappeared.

Carys looked at everyone, pleasantly surprised by the result of her efforts.

'But—where is the tiger?' Ben exclaimed, trying not to snigger.

Carys shaded her eyes with her hand and looked – and looked. The place where the figure had been was empty. There was nothing there at all.

'Perhaps the flash we saw was the sunlight playing tricks,' Ben said, scratching his head.

'Perhaps it was scared and ran away,' Izzy chuckled. 'I must say I don't think much of your magic, Carys.'

'Well, it must be somewhere,' Carys retorted. You saw the figure vanish. I expect it's gone into hiding.'

'Ow, c'mon, there's nowhere for it to hide out here on the beach,' Josh drawled, rolling his eyes.

'Well, I'm not going to go and look for it,' Carys replied crossly. 'Someone's sure to find it soon.'

'But for goodness sake, you can't leave a full-size tiger roaming about the beach. Suppose it attacked someone.'

'I don't care if it eats everyone, including *you*,' Carys retorted angrily, as she realized that her magic had once again not turned out the way she had anticipated. And with these words she got up and walked off in a huff with head held high.

The others looked after her, laughed and shrugged their shoulders.

'Let's say the 'thing' whatever it was, just vanished,' Josh said calmly. 'After all, it was only a blob on the horizon. 'No good worrying about it.'

'And the spell will wear off anyway after a while,' Izzy added. 'I imagine it was pretty harmless; more likely to be a pussy cat than a tiger.'

The boys nodded in agreement and the incident was soon forgotten.

2

Nothing more was heard about the unfortunate tiger episode, so it was assumed that the spell had indeed worn off before any damage was done.

A day or two later Carys decided to explore further along the coast where the cliffs looked more dramatic and plunged straight down into the sea. She found a cave and stood at the entrance looking out to the horizon but the combination of sunlight and waves soon made her eyes ache so she found a rock instead and sat watching the tide coming in. It was coming in fast, and she remembered being told that it could run faster than a galloping horse or a man could run. She shivered as she looked down at the water. It fascinated her; she liked it – and yet - and yet she couldn't swim. She mustn't let it get too close.

Very soon the sun began to lose its warmth and a damp chill took its place. Carys decided it was time to go. But as she attempted to stand she felt her foot slip from under her. It all happened so quickly she hardly had time to draw breath.

One moment she was on something solid, the next she was in the water. Down, down she went with the weight pressing on her until she couldn't breathe. There was no way up into the air. She panicked; words screamed inside her head but there was no air to form them.

Then when she felt she couldn't hold her breath a moment longer she heard a voice close to her. *Hold on to me* it said. And she felt something bearing her upwards towards the light, as the voice came again. *You're safe with me.*

She clung to the body which nudged, nosed, and propelled her along. And as she surfaced with a gasp that almost rent her in two, she saw who her rescuer was. Not a whale or a dolphin, but *a seal*. The creature kept her afloat until she reached the safety of the shore.

As she scrambled onto the beach and felt the shingles beneath her feet, she could see the seal watching her, head bobbing in the water keeping an eye on her.

Afterwards she wondered if she had imagined the voice. Was it from within her own head that the words had come when she felt death so close? Or *could* the seal have spoken to her? Either way, it had definitely saved her life.

......

She didn't know whether to tell the others about her ordeal. Most likely they wouldn't believe her. They would think it was just another of her mad stories made up to convince them that she was different. Well they knew that already. So she didn't say anything, but decided to visit the same part of the beach the next day just to see if that seal was anywhere around.

She set out early to make sure there was no-one about. Her mission must be secretive with nothing to frighten off her hoped-for visitor. She sat down on the towel she had brought, put on her sunglasses and looked out to sea. The early morning sun was hot, and she rolled over to one side into some shade. Gradually, despite her attempts to stay awake she began to doze. Time slipped by.

She was woken suddenly by the touch of something wet pushing against her and a tickling sensation against her bare feet.

Startled, she sat up and came face to face with a large grey seal who was winking at her with its dark inquisitive eyes.

The creature appeared not at all shy and in fact she concluded that it was those droopy long whiskers she could see which must have been tickling her feet.

'Oh, hello?' she exclaimed, not quite knowing in what manner one should address a seal.

A series of grunts came in reply, and then to her surprise the creature conducted itself in rather an unusual fashion by digging its flippers into the sand. It was not the usual procedure in which she had seen seals behave as they strove to push themselves across a beach.

Why was it doing this? Watching curiously, she then realized that it was trying to uncover something hidden there. Endeavouring to help, she scooped up handfuls of sand and stone and soon uncovered a long thin object made from some kind of hard substance.

Whatever could it be?

There was a pool close by into which she dipped it, swishing it around to clean off the sand whilst the seal watched her with obvious interest.

What was her astonishment then to discover that the item was a little instrument, a wind pipe made from a reed - but most amazing of all was the fact that she recognized it.

She would have known it anywhere. Hadn't she played a few notes on it herself a few years back? It belonged to the boy from the marsh, who with his friends Morgan and Kyle had become good friends of hers. *And his name was Finn.*

How had the seal known where it was - buried in the sand - unless it had put it there? Was the seal, in fact, Finn?

She stared at it with mounting excitement while the questions kept building inside her. Strangely enough since she'd heard the news of Finn's mysterious disappearance some years ago, she had often looked into the sea and seen seals bobbing up and wondered if Finn was among them.

As for the creature in question, having aroused her interest and seemingly rejoiced in it, the only thing apparently on its mind was to stretch out on its back and clap its flippers in the air.

She put her hand across her mouth to stifle a little burst of laughter. A sudden image of her friends' faces back at the camp site flashed before her. If only they could see her now, sitting beside a seal who was lying on its back in a state of such obvious ecstasy.

But the very thought of its happy state caused her to think again. From the account she'd heard of Finn's disappearance, assuming he was still alive, he must spend the greater part of his life at sea. This would explain his possible re-appearance as a seal, where he was at least able to venture on land now and again; and she was reminded of the many tales of the Selkie seal folk who were reputed to have been sighted in many parts.

Carys stared at the seal once again and held her breath. Then she uttered one word ... *Finn*. There could be no other explanation.

3

Carys came down to the beach every day after that. She was by now quite convinced that her theory was right. But she didn't tell her fellow travellers about what she had discovered or the story of Finn. It was almost certain they would never have believed her, but she decided to get in touch with Morgan and Kyle. They must be told and would know what to do.

But before she could act she had yet another surprise. Arriving at her usual time and place she noticed some lines scrawled on the sand. It was obvious that it had been written with some difficulty but the message spoke for itself:

Moon and magic, tide and sea
Hold and bind me. Set me free.
Free to roam the land I love
If not by land then air above.

Carys understood the first few lines. The Sea Witch held Finn by her magic of moon and tide, but the last line puzzled her. What did that mean? She couldn't wait to contact Finn's friends to ask for their help.

But this posed another problem. How to contact them? It was all very well to send Jac out with a message, as she did on occasions, but how would he know where to find them after so long?

Then she remembered something: crows could still recognize faces and memorize events up to a period of five years. Well, it wasn't quite as long ago as that. So it was worth a try.

Luckily Jac was still hanging around the camper-van at that time. He hadn't been used to captivity and was often away for weeks, being a free spirit. But he had never forgotten her kindness to him as a mother figure and they continued to be the best of friends.

Once back at the camp site, he alighted from the roof of the van and perched upon her shoulder. She whispered to him, and he pecked at her ear almost as if he were listening.

'Jac, dear, I have a mission for you. But how am I to give you directions of where to go?'

She frowned, thinking hard. Then an idea came to her: *Finn's reed pipe.* Why had she not thought of it before? Jac had heard Finn's performance when he sent them into what he called the Dreamworld. Jac had enjoyed his playing. But would he remember and associate it with Morgan and Kyle? There was a chance, but only a slim one. As far as she knew, the brother and sister were still living out on the marshes further along the coast with Finn's old grandmother in the same wood cabin.

She picked up the reed pipe and played a tune, not a very good one, since she had never mastered the trick. But what would Jac make of it? She knew he was listening intently by the way he cocked his head to one side.

And then he did a strange thing. He flew back onto the roof of the van and began a little dance, lifting up first one foot and then the other, just as if he were dancing. When he stopped he gave a series of little clicks and rattling sounds as if to say he understood perfectly what she wanted him to do.

Carys gave him a handful of his favourite peanuts. They often exchanged tokens, sometimes

Jac bringing her little gifts in the form of a button or a glass marble he'd found.

......

It was the early hours of the morning when Jac returned, and he perched on the camper roof making loud noises and waking everyone up.

Carys rushed outside and found one very wet and grumpy bird with feathers all awry, having been blown and battered by the wind. She got him inside and tried to dry him off with her hair dryer but he was most indignant at her efforts.

However she was relieved and delighted to find that the hoped for message was still intact.

See you soon. Thanks for directions.
Very excited! M and K

It was such a long time since they'd seen each other Carys was a little anxious as to how they might have changed. But she needn't have worried. Morgan was still the same confident character full of sensible bright ideas with Kyle fast following in her footsteps. When at last they had caught up with all the news, they had to be introduced to her three travelling companions. This was something she dreaded; things might be mentioned which were better left unsaid.

'Our friend Carys never fails to keep us entertained,' Ben grinned as they shook hands.

'Really?' Morgan exclaimed, looking at each in turn for an explanation.

'Don't take any notice of him,' Carys retorted, returning Ben's grin with an ominous glare. He noted her warning and no-one enlarged upon the subject, thankfully.

In any case Morgan and Kyle were too wrapped up in their own thoughts to give much attention to anything else. At the first opportunity they hurried off to the beach accompanied by Carys.

They waited for some time, but there was no sign of the seal. They were becoming more and more disappointed when their attention was drawn to a very large black-backed gull which alighted not far away and began drawing what looked like various shapes and symbols in the sand with its powerful beak.

'Whatever is it doing?' Kyle exclaimed, as he moved closer to get a better view.

The bird backed off as he approached and then settled on a nearby rock to watch. It was obvious that it wanted to gain their attention, and they wondered why.

All was explained when the symbols turned out to be letters - and formed the word *Finn.*

'He must have changed his shape to that of a bird. And I think I know why,' Carys laughed. 'Look how much easier it is for him to write with a beak rather than a flipper!'

'Wow, this is incredible!' Kyle cried, while Morgan clapped her hands with delight.

'A great black-backed gull is the biggest gull in the world,' Carys reminded them.

'Thanks for reminding us. But as long as Finn is still a creature tied to the sea I guess he can suit himself what form he takes,' Morgan replied. 'Now let's see how we can communicate. We know it's Finn, so he won't hurt us.'

They were reluctant to look into its eyes at first remembering the warning that most creatures took this as a threat. But the gull returned their stare boldly with dark, probing eyes, observing them intently as if searching their very souls.

'Finn, we've missed you so much,' Morgan whispered. And she was sure the bird winked at her before it strutted away.

'Now let's return to Finn's message,' Kyle said, growing impatient. 'The last line doesn't need much puzzling out, since Finn has changed from a seal. *If not by land than air above*, obviously refers to a bird.

Morgan nodded. 'The way I see it, Finn is now a kind of 'sea spirit' fated to haunt the sea-ways for the rest of his life – unless he can find this island which will somehow give him back his form allowing him to live again on land.'

'That's how it sounds,' Carys agreed, and then she pointed excitedly. 'Look! He's writing more in the sand – this time with that big sharp beak of his. How clever of him! What does it say?'

They stood on tip-toe, and craned their heads trying to see, as Finn struggled with the letters. The message was longer this time, so they had to wait patiently for him to finish before they were able to walk closer to look. And these were the words they read:

Look for an isle that vanishes
Just as you sight it there
Where magic lurks both high and low

Of which you must beware.
Find land the Sea Witch cannot take –
An island that will float
Blown by wind to hide in mist
That sails just like a boat.

'But of what must we beware? And what must we do, assuming one can reach this vanishing island?' asked the ever practical Morgan.

'Wait – look, there's more to come,' Carys said, pointing. And they craned forward to examine the four added lines Finn had scratched in the sand:

The dragon's pearl – to find it
Is the task you must perform
So the Sea Witch will reward me
And restore my voice and form.

'It's all very exciting,' Kyle remarked, having put their heads together and discussed it among themselves. But the general opinion was that they should sleep on it, and see if they came up with more ideas in the morning.

And as if to confirm this, the gull gave a loud trumpeting call and hastily took flight, winging its way back the way it had come across the sea.

4

There was no room in the camper for Morgan and Kyle, but as usual they had things well in hand, having brought their own tents which they set up close by.

The morning saw them all grouped together sharing breakfast beneath a shaded part of the cliffs overlooking the sea. Izzy had found a part-time job in a restaurant in the village a mile or two away and handed out fresh bread rolls while Ben and Josh cooked up some of the fish they'd caught the previous day.

Carys passed round shells and pebbles for her friends to see which she had painted in bright colours with mermaids, birds and fish. These she sold to tourists as a source of income.

But once Izzy and the boys had left to go their different ways, Morgan, Kyle and Carys turned their thoughts to more important things.

'How can we reach this elusive island, even assuming that we can find it?' Kyle asked.

'We'd find it quicker and easier if we could fly,' Carys replied rather unhelpfully.

'And since we can't, the obvious answer is by boat,' Morgan replied. 'But where do we get a boat? The boys need theirs for fishing, so that's out of the question.'

'I know of someone who keeps several and who will hire one out,' Carys exclaimed excitedly. 'He's a friend of mine - buys a few of my things and owes me a favour. I'll just tell him that we want to do some exploring round the coast. I know you and Morgan are good with boats.'

Carys disappeared to find the boat man, while Morgan and Kyle made their way to the beach hoping to find Finn. He was there waiting for them. No-one was about which was lucky, otherwise as Kyle pointed out it might look rather strange holding a one sided conversation with a gull.

'We have a problem,' Morgan frowned, as they crunched their way across the pebbles.

'What's that?' Kyle asked.

'How do we go about finding this mythical place. I can only *imagine* it.'

'Me too,' Kyle nodded. 'I see this island carried by the wind like a ship sailing to escape the clutches of the Sea Witch, making it almost impossible to land there. And *somewhere* … we don't know *where* … is a dragon … and a pearl.'

He looked across at the gull waiting to see if it would add anything to the story, but it stared fixedly straight ahead of them out to sea.

'It's easy to imagine the Sea Witch raising hurricanes and trying to snatch at bits of land that are always just out of reach,' Morgan continued. And then she stopped as a voice reached them, and they saw Carys running down the beach towards them.

'All settled,' she said, catching her breath. 'The boat will be ready early tomorrow morning.'

She had explained exactly what kind of boat she and her friends would need. Something solid and dependable, she said, since they had no idea of the conditions or sea miles they might have to navigate.

The vessel was a traditional fishing boat with a sail and a pair of oars.

'We haven't got many provisions,' Morgan

exclaimed, shaking her head. 'There isn't that much room in the boat.'

Kyle brushed such practicalities aside. 'Maybe our magic island will be nearer than we think.'

They made a list of certain items that came to mind, the most important being two tents, one for Kyle and one for the girls. Carys had left a note for the others at the camp to say they would be away for a few days.

She had deliberated whether or not to take Jac with her, and rather reluctantly decided against it. But to her surprise Jac had other ideas and clung obstinately to her shoulder when she tried to shake him off.

The others grinned when they saw him.

'You never know, he might come in useful,' they said.

'It will be a matter of the boat taking *us* somewhere rather than the other way round,' Morgan chuckled once they got aboard.

She was answered by a loud trumpeting call from Finn who had perched himself at the prow of the boat. Everyone laughed. Obviously he intended to point them in the right direction.

Kyle took his place at the helm while the girls grabbed the oars, and once they were clear of the shore they unfurled the sail.

Then Carys had an idea. 'I wonder what will happen if I play Finn's reed pipe,' she said. I can't make a tune but it may still hold some magic that will help us.'

Putting the pipe to her lips she was surprised at the sound it emitted: a soft haunting call that wafted across the waves.

Then several things followed in quick succession. Where there was previously only open sea the shape of an island appeared partly hidden beneath a curtain of blue mist, and at the same time a sound reached them across the water like that of a horn.

'What's that? Listen!' Kyle exclaimed.

'That's the sound of someone blowing on a conch shell,' Morgan exclaimed. 'I recognize the tone.'

As she spoke, they heard several splashes and a head popped out from the depths directly below them. At first they thought it must be a seal rising up from the shining water. But on looking closer they could see it was a boy from the aquatic race of Selkies. His skin was smooth like that of a seal and he stared up at them with big, round, liquid dark eyes.

5

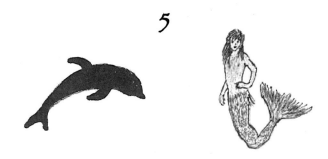

Another amazing thing was that the selkie boy could speak in a tongue they could understand.

'Hi, Land Legs!' he cried, which was obviously the name allotted to humans where he came from. 'Help me into your boat!'

So they lifted him up gently, marvelling at his soft seal skin and dark hair that reminded them of the weed that flowed with the surge of the tide. And as he gripped the side of the boat they could see that there were fine webs between all his fingers. His long fish's tail gleamed in the pale sunlight, making it difficult to understand that this was in truth a boy trapped within the skin of an animal.

When they asked his name, he told them he was called Shad, after a species of fish found in those parts. His voice came and went in short breaths as if echoing the rise and fall of the ocean. But his words were a warning of what lay ahead.

'Finn has asked me to be his voice,' he explained, 'since he cannot speak for himself. Everyone knows of the one who became a selkie and came to live with the sea people but who sometimes takes another shape. He is now *one who takes to the air ... one who leans on the wind*. You understand?'

They nodded, knowing this to mean what they already knew - that Finn had wings like a sea bird.

'I must tell you that yonder lies an island whose enchantment you must break if you are to bring Finn back to your world. I guess you already know that, but be assured there are many stories about islands like this. It's said a cave lies beneath the mountain where lives a dragon; that dragon carries a pearl between its teeth. Once the dragon is slain or vanquished the pearl must be cast into the sea, so releasing a mortal from the spell of the Sea Witch.'

But Kyle was only half listening. 'I often wondered if there might be some truth in the legends of merfolk. After all, we came from the sea, so why shouldn't some of us have adapted that way of life and decided to stay there.'

'What more do you know of this island?' Carys asked shyly, struggling to think of a question that might help them. 'Is it true that it floats?'

Shad nodded. 'It has been known to. Some say it's the top half of an underwater mountain. Those others of my kind won't go near it. The fire mountain has a loud voice that rumbles and roars. It throws down burning lumps of rock making the sea boil and smoke.'

'A volcano - you can imagine how angry that makes the Sea Witch,' Morgan exclaimed. 'So it's a dangerous place.'

'Quite so,' Shad agreed. 'And only at certain times does it allow entry; it hides under a curtain of thick mist, so no-one knows it's there. You were lucky to find it. But if you need me, remember to call me on the conch shell. Here … take it. Oh, and since you have the island in sight - look out for the Dragon's Teeth.'

'What are those?' Carys asked looking scared.

'Look!' exclaimed Kyle, pointing ahead at some rocks rising out of the sea. 'They're sharp and jagged like vicious teeth.'

He struggled to keep the boat on an even course, and so busy were they watching the rocks that they hardly noticed Shad slipping into the sea. When they next looked, he had disappeared.

'Blow, just when we could have done with some help,' Kyle muttered. 'Look how the breakers fling themselves against those rocks. Good name for them – dragon's teeth.'

The weather had changed and a big black cloud was filling the sky. Kyle soon had to shout to make himself heard above the slap of the boat on the water and the sound of the wind.

The girls struggled to take down the sail while Kyle barked out orders as he used all his strength to keep hold of the tiller.

Jac held on frantically emitting loud cawing cries, digging in his claws where he could, to stop himself from being blown away.

'What's that you've got in your hand, Carys?' Morgan asked, as she noticed a sheet of paper her friend was wrestling with.

'Oh, just a few things I wrote down from my grandmother's spell book which I thought might help in an emergency.'

Morgan was about to express her surprise at this announcement when there was an extra strong puff of wind and the paper was snatched away before she could speak.

'Away goes the spell!' Carys exclaimed distractedly. 'Oh, well, never mind. I don't expect it would have done much good anyway.'

Then Kyle suddenly gave a shout. 'Look at that ... a dolphin!'

They were amazed. They knew dolphins often followed boats, but they usually kept away in bad weather. The dolphin they could see ahead of them was obviously intent on guiding them in a different direction, and they watched as it shot into the air, keeping up a leaping and diving motion. Every so often it turned as if to make sure they were following before resuming its course.

'It's Finn. No doubt about it,' Carys cried excitedly. 'Shad wouldn't have been able to help ... but a dolphin ...' her voice trailed off.

Following in the wake of the dolphin they at last approached a part of the island which was friendlier. They were escorted quite close to the shore before the dolphin left them. He gave a whistle to announce his departure and everyone was quite convinced they saw him lift one flipper clear of the water in a sign of farewell.

Once they'd landed they set about finding a suitable place for their tent a good way from the beach. Then they had a look around. It was a little disappointing. The island seemed to just consist of stones and boulders with hardly any vegetation.

'Just a rocky wilderness,' Morgan said, with a shrug of her shoulders.

'But what shall we call it?' Carys asked. 'I think our island should have a name.'

The others pondered for a moment and then Kyle said, 'It shall be named *The Otherworld Island.* With all the legends we've heard, plus the bit about the fire dragon, it's definitely not of *our* world is it? He pointed towards the towering mass that loomed some distance away. 'I would guess that, as the lava from the volcano poured into the sea, the wind and waves forced it back and as it cooled it formed into those great, black jagged teeth that make it impassable from that side.'

'It's the age old fight between the land and sea, but the Sea Witch keeps rolling the dice so who knows which will win in the end,' Morgan added.

'The volcano might one day make more land,' Carys replied. 'That's if it doesn't disappear beneath the waves.'

This kind of conversation went on for some time, even after they had lit their camp fire and retired for the night. They hardly dared think what might await them the following day.

6

They were woken early in the morning by Jac's feet pattering over their heads and the low pitched call he gave on those occasions when his beak was closed, usually when he was anxious or alarmed.

Hurrying outside they discovered two things he had brought them: *a feather and a strand of hair*. They puzzled over this for some time without success.

'Is this a clue to warn us of something, Jac?' Carys asked. And as if in answer to her question, Jac gave an expressive squawk and watched them with his head on one side in a quizzical manner, as if to say *If I could speak I would tell you*.

He showed his agitation by flicking his tail and wings, prancing up and down, and fluttering back and forth in front of them; a trait Carys said he often practised when he needed to attract attention. It was obvious he wanted them to follow him so they decided to see where he would take them.

Before they did so however they took the precaution of alerting their friend Shad to let him know of their intentions. The 'fire mountain' as he called it, was silent for the moment, but they had no idea how long this might continue.

They had taken it in turns to practise their conch shell calls and considered themselves quite adept now, but the eerie sound echoing across the water never failed to fascinate them.

They were all for pushing the boat out to sea at first, but then Shad arrived before they had time to call more than once and they explained all about the strange offerings Jac had brought them.

Shad examined them carefully and he thought they came from the Weather Witch's cave on the part of the mountain that lay closest to them. Jac had obviously been exploring and brought things back from there which he thought might be of interest.

'Whatever is a Weather Witch?' Morgan wanted to know, and Carys said she used to hear her grandmother speak of such things years ago when she was little.

'It's an art that goes back hundreds of years,' she explained. 'Sailors would visit wind witches who sold them a rope or thread which had a few knots tied in it. They took them on all their voyages. You untied each knot to call on different weather patterns. They were spells or charms, isn't that so, Shad?'

The merboy nodded. 'The Weather Witch is named Marilla. She's a strange creature but she won't hurt you. Mind not to make her angry, though. They say she has a short temper. Oh, and by the way, the fire mountain is sleeping just now so it's safe for you to go there if you wish. But it's the home of the golden eagle, so be careful if you take Jac with you.'

With that, he took his leave of them.

It took them longer than they expected to reach the mountain on their side. But when they did so they had a surprise. A cavern appeared before them looking as though it had almost been hewn out of the rock. The robed figure of a woman stood at the entrance bent over a pot beneath which burnt a fire. And they knew this must be the mysterious Weather Witch, Marilla, of which Shag had spoken.

Intent upon stirring the contents of the cauldron with a long stick, she took no note of their presence despite the fact that she must have been aware of their presence.

When at last she looked towards them, they were able make out her gaunt features and keen hawk-like eyes. The intensity of her stare caused them to shiver slightly. And although she was facing the sun, she did not drop her gaze or turn away.

'I was expecting ye,' she said, in a high pitched voice reminiscent of some bird of prey. 'The work I do might be of some help to ye one day, but don't use my calling when out at sea, or 'twill be the worse for ye. Wait … and see.'

So saying, she raised her arm and pointed with her stick towards the sky, waving it three times in the air.

'Now listen …' she said.

They listened.

Marilla gave several piercing whistles, a common enough practice on land, but one which Morgan and Kyle had been warned never to use at sea for risk of calling up a storm. However what occurred next happened so quickly it took them completely off their guard.

In a few seconds there came an eerie howl turning to a roar as a rogue wind arose and fell upon them like a hungry wolf, tearing and ripping into them ruthlessly with its fangs.

'Watch out!' Kyle shouted, as they braced themselves and tried to shake off the ferocious attack. They attempted to grasp one another, but were sent spinning and whirling like leaves against the rocks at the entrance of the cave.

It was all over before they could right themselves, but so sudden had been the onslaught that they were left shaken and gasping for breath.

'Now you see what power Marilla commands,' the woman declared. 'Be careful not to step this way again or it might be worse for ye.'

She appeared to hesitate for a moment as if undecided whether to speak more, then turned to Carys and asked a question.

'What magic do you have about ye, child?'

'None,' Carys replied evasively.

'Yet I mind ye do - when the urge takes ye.'

Carys felt herself grow red with embarrassment, and she wondered how Marilla could know so much. She was saved further questions when Jac, who had perched out of the way keeping a wary eye on things, fluttered down to perch on her shoulder.

'Ah, here's the one who dared pluck hair from Marilla's head; a stranger to these parts,' the witch exclaimed. 'Well, my pretty, we don't have crows around 'ere. Just wait 'til the golden eagle sets eyes on ye. Reckon ye'll soon be snapped up as a tasty morsel.'

'I knew he shouldn't have followed us,' Carys whispered worriedly to the others. 'I don't think we should stay here long.'

Marilla heard her. 'Just long enough to watch 'ow my magic works,' she retorted. 'Jac will be safe enough in my shelter. The eagle daren't mess with *me*.'

It was at this point that they noticed several small gulls strung up by their legs on a wire, and realized it must have been from one of these that Jac snatched the feather to show them.

Marilla's eyes were sharp. She noticed where they looked, and smiled. 'Ah, only a few left to do my bidding, but 'ave no fear. Now they only sleep.'

Next they watched in a kind of horror as she dipped her hands into the boiling liquid in the cauldron allowing it to run over her wrists. Yet she uttered not a sound, and her hands when she withdrew them were unharmed as she held them up in front of her. She then took hold of a long piece of cord which she pulled from a pile nearby, holding it firmly between her fingers. She then proceeded to tie three knots into it, muttering to herself as she did so. They could just about catch her words:

> *'Twist and tangle, knot and twine,*
> *Make wind of storm or weather fine.'*

She then paused for a moment and began again in a different tone of voice:

> *'By the knot of one, this spell is begun,*
> *By the knot of two, the spell comes true;*
> *By the spell of three ...'*

She stopped before she completed the sentence; looked up, and gave them a toothy grin. 'That last is at someone's peril.'

It was then she endeavoured to explain the

procedure, telling them that her 'customers' once used to call at the island before it became too dangerous for their ships to land. Sea captains as well as sailors used the charms for guidance. 'Witch's ropes' they called them. A single knot called up a gentle breeze, two for a fair wind, and three knots to summon a storm. The third knot was always a risk that might cause a boat to capsize.

'Thank you for telling us of the magic you make with the winds,' Morgan said politely, 'but how do you manage now when ships no longer call here.'

'Ah, I make the gulls work for me,' Marilla replied. And she went on stirring something in the cauldron before her without offering more explanation.

'You wonder what I am boiling away at,' she said at last, without looking up. 'Well, see 'ere.' She pointed to a pile of shells that had previously lain unnoticed.

'Mussels, whelks, cockles and clams,' Kyle exclaimed, looking more closely. 'We used to collect many of those at one time.'

'Indeed,' Marilla grinned. 'I remember they

were a favourite dish when you lived out on the marshes with Finn.'

'How did you know …' Kyle began. Then bit his lip. Her words came as no great surprise, since the unexpected was becoming an almost normal occurrence by now.

'Ah,' Marilla smiled. 'The Sea Witch … you were led here because of her magic of moon and tide. Mine is of the Air … more reliable. But one must know how to fight magic with magic.' She continued with her stirring, and this time she crooned a little rhyme as she did so.

> *'Water bubble, swirl and churn,*
> *Stew and simmer each in turn;*
> *Winkles, whelks and cockles all,*
> *Big 'uns, salty, gritty, small.'*

'Marilla has special bags she keeps for those who do not obey her,' she went on. 'Stray winds, you might say.' She pointed towards the cave and shook her head, then went on mumbling to herself.

'What did you say about the gulls?' Morgan asked, remembering how she had spoken of them previously.

'They come seawards when they're called. On the far side of the mountain they *won't* come. On that side lives the golden eagle that would prey on them. They carry my spell threads out to the ships and each gull stays only a few hours until the spell has worked out. Then it will fly free.'

'But how do you know which ships are which?' Carys asked, surprising herself with her boldness.

This question seemed to annoy the Weather Witch, who frowned and replied 'That's my secret.' She stared at Carys with a peevish expression, and Carys was reminded of Shad's warning that Marilla had a short temper.

'Too many questions to be asking a body,' she exclaimed. Hadn't I told ye enough already, my young friend? A little wisdom that's all ye has. And that little has a habit of going astray. Is that not so? Watch thy tongue, young lady, and see it doesn't run away with ye in future.'

Before any of them had time to draw another breath, a sound reached them that grew louder by the second. It was a rogue wind that appeared from nowhere, and Marilla clicked her fingers in the air and spoke to it.

'Ye are a wind that blows hot and cold, so 'tis thy turn to go into one o' the bags, but now ye must wait a while in the queue. Carys will go into the bag to remind her of being respectful to witches - since she wishes to be one herself.'

Morgan and Kyle stared in awe at Carys. Did she really aspire to witchcraft? They knew she was capable of certain things; that her grandmother had a book of spells in which she was interested. But they knew little more.

All that was certain at the moment was that Carys was in trouble. The next thing they heard were her cries for help emanating from somewhere inside the cave.

To their horror they saw Marilla taking a large needle with a thread attached to sew up the bag in which Carys was imprisoned.

'Just to make sure she won't escape for the time being,' she told them.

7

Morgan and Kyle were completely at a loss to know what to do next. They couldn't think about trying to help Carys with Marilla so close at hand. But their problem was answered almost directly as the Weather Witch took up a large net from behind some rocks.

'I must go out and catch me more messengers,' she muttered, looking skywards. 'When I call they come, and then I trusses 'em up ready to do my work. I just breathes on 'em, and they stops their flutterin' and strugglin' straight away.'

Morgan and Kyle couldn't help suppressing a shudder. It seemed so callous. However it would give them the chance they wanted once she was out of the way.

She turned her back on them, and was just about to go about her business when she caught hold of one of the cords from a pile nearby, holding it out towards Morgan.

'Here's a gift for ye. I know what ye'll be thinking; Finn can do what I can, without my bit o' rope. That's as may be, but it's as well to mind what I told ye: to make a spell untie the knots – one for a breeze - two for a fair wind - three for a storm. It might be useful to ye, one o' these days. Now just be off, unless ye wants to end up in t' sack.'

She shooed them away with a few disgruntled words moving off in the direction of the seashore. Kyle kept a watch until she was out of sight, and then he and Morgan returned to Carys.

She was still in a state of shock at being confined in such a small space, but she had made a tiny hole in the cord bag with the sharp end of a pin. Placing her mouth over the hole she gave a sharp whistle. This alerted Jac, who was hovering outside.

'One of us had better keep a watch in case Marilla returns,' Morgan pointed out. So Kyle ran back to keep a look-out.

'How bad is it in there?' Morgan asked, in what she hoped was a loud enough voice. 'Is it difficult to breath?'

'Not too bad,' a muffled voice replied. 'But it's so dark.'

Jac meanwhile knew at once what was expected of him and pecked away furiously with his sharp beak. It took only a few moments for him to tear a hole in the thick sacking.

'Clever boy,' Morgan enthused. And she called out to ask Carys if she could help in making the hole bigger.

'I'm trying, but it's not easy. The sacking is so tough.'

'Wait a moment, let me look round to see if there's anything here that might be useful,' Morgan said. And she began poking among the nets and fishing tackle littered around the cave. There were the inevitable hooks with lines which she discarded, and then she came across a spear type weapon; a wooden shaft with a pointed head. Obviously the Weather Witch must use this on those occasions that suited her. But it was just the thing which would solve the problem.

Morgan shouted out a warning to Carys to be careful as she prodded the spear into the hole. It didn't take long and Carys soon found she was able to scramble out.

'Hurry, I believe she might be coming back!' Kyle shouted. 'I can see a dark cloud in the distance coming closer.'

They could feel the temperature had suddenly changed. A cold draught began to sweep towards them causing them to shiver.

Carys caught hold of Morgan's hand, and with one accord they raced out to join Kyle behind some rocks that lay close by.

Just in time. With a whirl of her dark robe, Marilla swept into the cave, her net full of small gulls that were stretched out as if asleep.

She began talking to them in soft tones as she sorted them out, stringing them up by their legs ready to join those on her 'fishing line', as Morgan described it afterwards.

'Now you just wait a little my dears, an' no harm will come to ye.'

They left her muttering to herself as they crept away, unable to believe they had escaped so easily. It was all very well for Shad to assure them that they were in no danger in the Weather Witch's domain, but they would far rather not take any chances.

8

Luckily the three of them had no difficulty in surviving on those provisions they found around them. They searched for driftwood along the shore by day and lit fires whenever the need arose. They cooked fish which they caught with hook and line from their boat and used fresh water from a mountain spring for drinking.

Jac roosted most of the time on top of a tent pole. He was supposed to be on guard, but Carys told how crows never made any sound at night so it was only in the early evening or morning he would be of use.

They were wise to be wary since anything might confront them they were unprepared for, and they found themselves almost on the point of waiting for the unexpected to happen. The sight and sound of the nearby 'fire mountain' with its rumbling and grumbling and occasional smoke signals also did nothing to inspire confidence. They were afraid to camp too close or too far from the sea, and as a precaution their tents were pitched high up on the beach. At night the tent flaps were not only fastened but zipped up tightly to guard against possible predators.

But this was hardly enough for the terrifying event about to reveal itself. Luckily for them the intruder decided to make an entrance in the early evening, and Jac at once sounded the alarm.

The three of them decided it would be safer to assemble out in the open where they could see what was going on. At first they could hear only a slow shuffling of sand and stones like the wind blowing up the beach rattling the pebbles and kicking up the sand. But Jac would not warn them for nothing, and they were aware some danger was imminent.

They didn't have long to wait. A creature that resembled a large crocodile suddenly emerged from behind one of the tents and came lumbering towards them. Except that it was not a crocodile - having two tusks or horns protruding from either side of its head.

'Gee, what on earth does *that* call itself,' Kyle exclaimed.

'This is Otherworld Island,' Morgan reminded him. 'Things are obviously different here.'

The creature suddenly stopped short in its tracks and stared at them unblinkingly, as if uncertain what to make of them.

The three of them stared back. Just the sight of its big yellow eyes glinting greedily was enough to send shivers down their spines.

'Back away slowly; don't make any sudden movements,' Carys whispered. 'I've seen how Jac stays very still and just clicks with his beak whenever danger threatens.'

But the creature clearly had other plans. Without warning it made a rush at them, gnashing its teeth, hissing and snapping.

'Run! Run fast!' Morgan urged, pushing Carys in front of her. 'Crocs can run as fast as a man, if that's what it is.'

Kyle turned in his flight to grab handfuls of sand which he threw into the eyes and mouth of the oncoming monster, but this only temporarily blinded it and gained but a few seconds.

His mind was racing. Who could they call for help? Shad would be of no use – not this time.

And then, just as the thought came to him, his attention was drawn to a loud, shrill cry accompanied by the beating of wings - and a sudden streak of black and white flashed between Kyle and his oncoming predator.

Finn! His powerful sixth sense was well known. But what could he do in his present form against such an adversary?

Finn however had something they had not reckoned on. In his present form he was in possession of a sinister weapon – a cruel and vicious sword – his powerful long pointed beak.

In one determined move the gull dive-bombed the surprised monster taking it completely off its guard, and aiming at its eyes.

Kyle watched, as did the others who had paused in their flight.

The move was both quick and effective. With a concentrated effort the great gull slashed, thrust and jabbed at the monster's eyes, blinding both at the same time.

Morgan and Carys turned and returned to the scene, staring with a mixture of shock and relief as the monster roared in anger and turned away towards the sea, whether from habit or instinct they were unsure.

The great gull hovered for a few moments above them, while Morgan, Carys and Kyle waved their thanks. Then it also made for the open sea.

'Wow! What an awe inspiring experience,' Kyle exclaimed. 'I'd never have believed it, had I not been there.'

'Awe inspiring is one way of looking at it,' Carys gasped. 'I'm still out of breath – not used to running that fast. Let's hope there are no more such surprises in store.'

9

Up to now they seemed to have had little chance to properly explore the small island in order to discover the dragon's cave.

They decided to remedy this the very next day, being careful to leave Jac behind on account of Marilla's warning of the eagle who nested on that side of the mountain.

Morgan and Kyle were puzzled as to how exactly they were to stop Jac from following them, but Carys explained that the procedure was simple. She just shooed him away – much to his indignant surprise. But he was a wise bird, like all those of his family, and if his adopted mother figure did not wish him to accompany her for whatever reason, then he was quite prepared to resign himself to the fact.

'I don't see how the eagle can be a danger to us,' Carys remarked, as they got ready to set out. 'Eagles nest high up and we'll be way down below the mountain.'

'Exactly what I thought, but things here are not the same as we know them. Think of the croc with horns! I reckon we should get a message to Finn to let him know what we intend doing.'

'Good idea,' Morgan nodded, reaching for the conch shell which they kept close at hand.

They met Shad at the far end of the beach, a place he preferred where there were some rocks and pools he could hide amongst should the need arise.

'I don't know much about eagles,' he admitted, when they told him of their plans. 'Except that the gulls keep away from them. But a gull the size of Finn might be different.'

'Very different,' Morgan added, much to everyone's surprise. Being the eldest and more informed about things, she considered herself quite useful when it came to general knowledge. 'A great gull like Finn – the biggest of all - has even been mistaken for an albatross, so I was told. Did you know,' she continued, 'that gulls often attack whales?'

'And they fight eagles,' Kyle added.

'Exactly,' Morgan replied, looking a little miffed at Kyle's quick response.

He went on to remark that his sister only knew stuff about gulls because she was always watching them at sea when they joined with the crews on the fishing boats.

'But gulls are gulls, whatever kind,' Morgan insisted. 'All have the same traits; they're all completely fearless. It's their bravery that's scary.'

'I wish we had a map,' Kyle sighed, changing the subject and scratching his head.

'Yes, how are we to find this cave?' Carys replied. 'We could be looking for days, and Shad can't help us on this one.'

'We'll just have to search, won't we?' Morgan answered a little impatiently, 'unless Finn knows the way.'

But there was no sign of Finn, and so they set off in the opposite direction to that which they took upon meeting with the Weather Witch.

Once they left the shore their path was strewn with rocks and boulders and they had to pick their way carefully. The going got rougher the further they went.

'Look!' Carys cried suddenly, pointing above them. And staring upwards they caught sight of an eagle circling and then hovering motionless in the air. As they watched, it came closer, until it had alighted on a nearby crag where it surveyed them with sharp, beady eyes.

'It looks like it's daring us to venture further into its territory,' Kyle whispered urgently. 'What do we do now?'

'Nothing … while we think,' Morgan replied, a little nervously.

But they were given little chance to think. The eagle appeared to poise itself ready to launch an attack. And then to their surprise Carys pushed herself forward, gave a command, and pointed her finger at a rocky ledge a little above where the eagle was crouched.

There came a sudden rumble followed by a crash and several stones came rolling down in quick succession. The eagle, which had already begun its descent from the rocky outcrop, veered off sharply just in time to avoid being struck.

'Whew! How did you do that?' Kyle gasped, while Morgan stared at her dumbfounded.

'Do what? Oh, that … that was just …'

'We know,' Kyle interrupted with a grin. 'It was just something you saw your grandmother do once.'

'That was amazing! It saved us from a nasty situation,' Morgan exclaimed. 'But I'd like to know how you did it.'

Carys laughed. 'My grandmother was good at tricks like that, but I think the skill slipped a generation somewhere.'

Just as she said this, a shadow passed over them and they made out the shape of another large bird overhead.

'It's Finn!' Carys exclaimed in relief, glad that she didn't have to go into any more detail regarding her unpredictable use of magic.

Soaring to a great height, the gull gave harsh and loud cries as it swept along in a calm majestic flight, moving in ever widening circles.

Morgan shaded her eyes with her hand, as she stared upwards. 'You can see how it looks a bit like an albatross from a great distance.'

They watched, thrilled, as an epic fight between the two birds began. Like the eagle, Finn rode the wind to circle high above the mountain and then swiftly swooped lower to make a series of dive attacks on its adversary.

In response the eagle altered its direction and began to swiftly twist and turn in order to defend itself. Then a desperate engagement took place.

High pitched whistling calls from the eagle could be clearly heard above the cry of the gull, which took a short circle round it until its head and tail were in direct line. It then made a desperate stoop and struck the eagle on its back, causing it to wheel and turn as quickly as its large and heavy wings would allow. By attacking from behind in this way the gull managed to harass the eagle and engage it for some time.

The real danger was the eagle's lethal talons stretched out before it, ready to snatch and grasp. Once they got a grip on the gull, it seemed all would be lost. On the other hand, powerful bird of prey though it was, the eagle had to fight hard to grab the gull whilst it jabbed at it with its sharp beak. In several daring moves the gull seemed to almost ride on the back of the eagle in a death defying bid to scare it off.

And all the time, Morgan, Kyle and Carys watched half in awe, half in horror, as the battle unfolded before them. It might have lasted longer than it did, but for the desperate loud cries of the gull which had unexpected results.

It seemed that Finn had been heard by others of his kind and reinforcements were on their way. As they watched, the sky became filled with gulls of all sizes.

And even when the eagle was outnumbered by about a hundred to one, it still fought viciously. But eventually it began making several short flights from rock to rock, and then flew off further along the coast until it was out of sight.

The three of them watching couldn't honestly say they were sorry to see the end of it, although they felt sure there must have been much that was not accounted for.

And after all that, they were still no wiser as to the whereabouts of the dragon's cave. They were forced to admit that their search would have to wait for yet another day.

10

The drama that had played itself out in the skies above her, still continued to weigh on Morgan's mind. True, it had ended well for Finn, but she had to ask herself how the ordeal would have affected him and also what injuries he had sustained.

She decided she needed a few moments to herself and wandered off to listen to the whisper of the waves along the shore, the sound of which she found oddly comforting.

It was therefore a considerable shock to catch sight of the gull, the subject of her thoughts, perched above a nearby pool, staring down at something directly below it with fierce intensity.

'Finn … 'the word froze on her lips. Catching her breath, she stopped herself just in time. Her presence seemed such an intrusion; the creature before her suddenly appearing so vulnerable compared to herself. How bruised and battered it must be ... and tired. It obviously needed to rest.

She noticed that occasionally it bent to peck at something in the water which she imagined must be a small fish or crab stranded by the tide. Her curiosity aroused, she sidled closer and could just make out the last of the sunlight striking the surface of the pool.

At last she was able to reach out and gently smooth the bird's ruffled feathers. And as she did so, she became suddenly aware of the smear of blood on its white head.

'Oh, Finn,' she exclaimed, and quickly wetted her handkerchief to wipe away the stain.

The bird allowed her to do this, but continued staring into the pool. Morgan followed its gaze and gave a gasp at the reflection before her. It was the same image she remembered when she had stayed with Finn on the saltmarsh a few years ago. *It was the face of the Sea Witch.*

And the sound that reached her was like that of the wind as it murmured and played along the shore - but which now came as words:

Fly with the wind, Finn. Lean on the wind.

She's mocking him, Morgan thought; telling him that he must remain as a sea bird. And a sense of anger passed through her. Leaning over, she whispered a few words of comfort to the bird, which is all she felt she could do.

'It might take a little time, Finn dear, because even when we *do* find the dragon's cave, we have to discover *where* the pearl is. But have no fear - we won't fail you.'

......

Yet she could not rid herself of the image. The Sea Witch could change to suit herself, so how could they trust her? But she also had a softer side. Morgan had watched as baby seals struggled to overcome their fear of water before they could swim, and how the Sea Witch opened her arms gently to gather them in. She was unpredictable, wild and tempestuous, but she was also a life force – a shape changer. She was fond of games, especially ones she knew she could win.

But maybe this time would be different.

11

Kyle was woken early the next day by the sound of waves crashing on the shore. The storm that had been threatening the previous evening had worsened.

Without waking the girls, he dressed hurriedly and having decided that the tents were pitched high enough up the beach to be under no threat, was just about to retrace his steps when he happened to glance out to sea.

The sight that met his eyes caused him to look once, twice, and a third time, just to be sure. Was he dreaming? There was a ship – no mistaking it - in full sail riding high on the waves making straight for the Dragon's Teeth.

He rushed to tell the girls, who scrambled out from their tents and ran with him down to the beach.

'It's a mirage – it must be,' Morgan cried, shielding her eyes with her hand against the glare of the sun.

'Yes, it's a trick of the mist and sunlight making shadows on the water,' Carys agreed.

'No, no. It's *real*,' Kyle insisted, 'as real as I'm standing here. And it's heading for the rocks. The current's very strong there, it will draw them in. We have to warn them!' He began leaping up and down, shouting and waving his shirt, which he had torn off in his excitement. 'Hard to port!' he yelled.

'They can't hear anything above the storm – and they're too far away,' Carys said, turning to Morgan.

But Kyle continued to wave and shout.

'It's from force of habit,' Morgan said, shaking her head. 'No use telling him.'

They remained watching, and were relieved to see that just when it seemed certain it must hit the rocks, the ship managed to slip past them towards the shore.

Morgan put out a hand to restrain her brother. 'Leave it, Kyle. We don't know *who*, or *what* they might be. They could be unfriendly – dangerous even

To her relief, Kyle nodded. 'S'pose you're right.'

'We'll just have to watch and wait for a while,' Morgan continued. 'Don't forget ...'

'I know what you're going to say,' Kyle interrupted. 'Don't forget this is Otherworld Island.

'Exactly.'

'They could be pirates,' Carys suggested, which caused a smile.

......

But it turned out that's exactly what they were, and they discovered this in rather a strange way.

The ship had anchored just off the shore in a sheltered cove; Kyle had watched a rowing boat carry four of the crew to shore.

'I made sure I was well hidden,' he reported, 'but I wanted to see what kind of people they were, and if they were likely to pose a threat. They looked a rough lot, so I was wise not to approach. They made camp at the entrance of a small cave where they stored some of their gear, then lit a fire, and sat around making a lot of noise, laughing and drinking.'

The girls gave Kyle a lecture for taking such a risk, but were intrigued at the same time.

'Did you hear anything that might give a clue as to their intentions?' Morgan asked.

'I don't expect you were close enough for that, were you?' Carys added, as she tried to imagine the scene Kyle described.

'As a matter of fact, I was,' he replied with a grin. 'I heard quite a lot, especially as they were singing in such loud voices. The song wasn't long - I remember the words.'

'Really?' Morgan couldn't hide her surprise. 'Well, don't keep us in suspense.'

'It went like this,' Kyle said, assuming an air of some importance:

Yo ho ho,
Let the wild winds blow,
We're ne'er afeard
Of friend or foe;
Our booty waits
In a place we know
In a mountain of fire
In a cave below
Where a king still sleeps
From the long ago.

This caused a lot of interest and controversy, as Kyle knew it would. It appeared that the suggestion the intruders might be pirates was a strong possibility. The intriguing bit was the reference to a place 'in a mountain of fire' - the volcano - and the cave which lay below it. But how did these men know about it? And what did they mean by the words 'where a king still sleeps from the long ago.' What king? If it was from long ago, then he must be dead.

They found it all most exciting if a little puzzling.

'What about asking Shad if he can help?' Carys asked. 'He says none of the mere people have ever visited the cave and he doesn't know where it is, but he might have some knowledge of the legend surrounding the king who's buried there.'

'Good idea,' Kyle replied at once, and Morgan agreed, so they decided to call Shad on their conch shell, now referred to as 'the one way telephone'.

12

But before they could call Shad, they had a surprise visitor. One of the crew from the ship arrived, who had obviously been patrolling the beach to report on any intruders.

He was a rough looking fellow wearing an eye-patch, having brown rotten teeth and a dirty bandana tied round his head. Large gold ear-rings hung from each ear.

At first he was suspicious of why they were there, and of their intentions. 'What you doin' 'ere?' he shouted.

Morgan sauntered over to him assuming a confidence she was far from feeling, having whispered to the others to keep a low profile. If he thought they were just a few innocent youngsters loafing around, he might leave them alone.

'We got washed ashore in a sudden storm,' she said, remembering how the pirate ship had just missed the rocks themselves. 'We haven't been here long and don't intend to stay; just waiting till our things dry out. We're thinking of doing a bit of fishing,' she added, adopting an off-hand attitude.

'Know anythin' about this 'ere place?' the man asked.

Morgan shook her head, as did the others.

'Rum sort o' place. You b'n poking around?'

'Oh no,' Kyle replied, speaking for the first time. 'We're a bit scared of going far. It looks too spooky.' He pointed towards the forbidding mountain in the distance.

'Ooh aye, that there be a devil … a fire devil. Just rose up out o' sea one day, 'tis said. Shakes the whole place an' throws down red 'ot rocks. Could come tumblin' down on ye. Don't ye go wanderin' 'ereabouts,' he said, shaking his head; ''tis not safe for young uns. Bad things live in t' caves.'

'What kind of things?' Carys asked timidly.

'Why, things loik them big critters in books: sea monsters an' bats an' snakes. You best go on an' leave this place quick.'

'He's warning us off all right, Carys whispered to Morgan, 'and we know why.'

The man noticed her muttering beneath her breath, and turned to her with an oily smile. 'I see yer bin loiking at me black eye-patch, m'dear. Don't scare ye, do it? Only one eye I 'ave, but that's a *good* un. Ye can't 'ide from the loikes o' me.' And he tapped his other eye.

Carys shuddered.

He waited a moment to make sure his words had taken effect. 'I be a pirate ri't enough. But there aint enough ships t' plunder these days.'

'There you are, I *told* you they were pirates,' Kyle whispered, cupping his hand over his mouth.

'Ssh, he'll hear you,' Morgan warned.

But the pirate pretended he hadn't heard. 'We bin voyaging fer months – *years*, we 'ave. And we'd 'eard as 'ow there was an island like this 'ereabouts. Well, wouldn't yer loik to find a place no-one knowd about?'

'That might depend on what dangers one might have to face,' Morgan reminded him. 'It's not much good getting killed just to discover a new island.'

'Ah, that's what I bin saying to t' others,' the pirate corrected himself. 'But we be used t' danger, me 'arties; dangers be all in t' course of things fer us, but 'tis not for young uns.'

He then went on to let slip something that sounded more interesting.

'There were a job us came to do when we was 'ere before. But that there devil nearly blew, so us 'ad to get out quick, like.'

He left them with a warning about a sea dragon that had its den in one of the caves.

''ope ye've got more 'n a bow an' arrow to defend yerselves with,' he leered as he at last turned his back on them.

They were quite relieved when he had stomped off further along the beach. And as soon as he was out of sight, they called Shad. There were so many questions they hoped he could help them with.

13

Once Shad made an appearance they related all that the pirate had told them, including the pirate song on the beach which Kyle had overheard, and some intriguing words about the island.

'Legend tells that it just rose up out of the sea one day, Carys said. 'I didn't know islands did that.'

'Volcanic ones do,' Morgan replied. 'They can appear from nowhere.'

'And disappear,' Kyle added. 'The Sea Witch would have no trouble swallowing one.'

'Not with us still on it, I hope,' Carys retorted.

But Kyle was thinking about the pirates. 'We know that they've been here before; that they had to leave in a hurry and didn't get what they came for. All we have to do is follow them,' he stated emphatically.

'*You'll* follow them, you mean,' Morgan replied with a toss of her head. 'It's a male thing, isn't it … getting to do all the exciting bits?'

'I agree,' Carys nodded. 'But it makes sense. More than one of us is bound to draw attention.'

'Mm, point taken,' Morgan grinned. 'And *I'm* usually the practical one.'

Shad, who had been listening in silence, suddenly decided it was time to explain a little more of the puzzle surrounding the dragon and the subject of the 'booty' which the pirates had boasted of, in their song.

'I've asked around, and no-one seems to know much,' he announced. 'But you might find this interesting: there's a curse on the spot where the king is buried. He lived long ago when the island was much bigger, before the fire mountain blew half of it apart. No-one knows his name, but anyone robbing the tomb is sure to come to a bad end. It's just a legend — like the crown said to be buried with him.'

Kyle whistled. 'A *crown* — so that's what they're after: the treasure of a king's crown.

There was an awed silence.

Then Morgan spoke. 'Of course it goes without saying; evidently this crew heard the story and decided to go and try their luck.'

'Can't blame them I suppose … since they're pirates, I mean,' Kyle added hastily.

'So the dragon guards both the crown *and* the pearl,' Carys said slowly. 'And the Sea Witch makes the pearl the main objective because she knows it's almost impossible to get hold of.'

'That way, she can keep Finn in her clutches forever,' Morgan concluded. Then a thought struck her. 'But how will we know when the pirates intend to set out for the cave?'

'That's easy,' Shad replied. 'I'll get some of my friends to hang around their ship. The crew are always going backwards and forwards with supplies. One of us is bound to hear what they've got planned. I'll let you know as soon as I learn anything. And another thing - there's only four of them altogether.'

Kyle grinned at that. 'I guess it will take at least four of them to overcome a dragon.

14

It was pretty certain that once their visitor had reported that the coast was clear, the pirates would lose no time in making their move. So the appearance of Shad arriving to inform that the four men were gathering a few things together in readiness for their trip was not surprising.

What *did* surprise them was the fact that Finn appeared as Kyle was preparing to leave. Jac had already decided to accompany him, having flown onto his shoulder. But having taken one glance at the big gull, the crow quickly disappeared from view.

Carys laughed. 'Jac is taking no chances with Finn around,' she said. 'But Finn will prove much more useful.'

The thought of having Finn as both guide and companion was one that left Kyle feeling both relieved and thankful. But by the time they had caught up with the four men, he was already finding things a little strange.

He seemed to have been climbing upwards for some time, yet actually covering little ground. The total land mass was only a few miles across he guessed, so how could this be? Thinking he must be dreaming, he stopped for a moment to shade his eyes against the sun. He tried to think logically but could make no sense of it; then remembered that it was he, himself, who had named the place 'Otherworld Island'. He came to the conclusion that it was all to do with the magic surrounding it, which wouldn't bear too much thinking about anyway.

Luckily Finn was a good guide, always keeping in sight, always a little ahead of him. And at last having clambered over more and more fallen boulders until his legs began to ache, he reached a cave set into the rock. At first sight it appeared little more than a big fissure but this was a good enough reason he guessed for it to have remained so well hidden. Obviously it must widen out somewhere at some point, but many seeking the whereabouts of such a place would have passed it without a second glance.

He hid himself behind one of the many large rocks, so he could see all that passed.

The men were busy with a big fishing net, a

bucket, spade, and several formidable weapons. Finn had positioned himself a very short distance away observing all that passed, but of course no-one took the slightest notice of a nosy gull.

As the pirates disappeared inside, Kyle managed to sidle closer to get a better view. At first he found it difficult to focus until his eyes grew accustomed to the half-light that filtered in from outside. Then he could see that the cave widened out to form a kind of tunnel gouged and etched out either by lava or water, he was not sure which.

He watched with interest, wondering what the men had in mind. How did they intend to dispatch the dragon to get to the tomb? And more important – where *was* the dragon?

As if in answer, a sudden roar came to his ears. This was followed by another, louder, and more terrifying one, and there rose up a huge sea monster covered with shining scales. It towered over the men who tried to attack it using hand to hand combat, thrusting and slashing in an attempt to pierce its armour plating. Their weapons, Kyle noticed, were no more than old-fashioned cutlasses, making it necessary for them to advance quite close to the creature in order to do much harm. But they were nimble and quick, and managed to use the strategy of dodging and circling their opponent, which, as it happened, only appeared to make the creature madder than ever.

First of all there were all four of them engaged in this battle game, and the use of the big net became obvious when it was thrown over in an attempt to entangle and imprison the monster in its mesh. After this had been tried with little effect, the bucket was brought into play, and Kyle saw that they threw sand into the creature's eyes in an attempt to temporarily blind it.

Most of the time there appeared to be only three of the men engaged. Another seemed to have disappeared somewhere at the back of the cave, and when he eventually emerged, he was carrying a sack. Turning to the rest of the crew he delved into it and held up the trophy they had come for.

Although he was some distance away, Kyle was just able to catch a glimpse of the beautiful object: a crown of gold. Even in the dim light the stones with which it was set, sparkled and gleamed.

There was an instant cheer from the others, who at once left off tormenting the dragon.

And then, without warning, a sudden pulse shook the ground and a rumble echoed through the cave followed by a shower of small stones that came pattering down.

The men stopped dead in their tracks and began to shout. 'The volcano! Quick! Out! Out!'

And they came scrambling into the open, one after the other, looking neither to right or left.

Kyle stood still, too terrified to move. But Finn gave a loud cry and landed heavily upon his shoulder. The sudden impact roused him to action and he began to stumble away from the danger that threatened as fast as his shaking legs would allow. But the sudden rumblings and grumblings from the volcano appeared to be one of its very infrequent outbursts that were thankfully soon over.

The path back to familiar territory however, proved as perplexing as the journey Kyle had undertaken to get there. How would he ever remember any of it, in order to retrace his steps? Finn was the answer. Only Finn would know the way. But why then had he not led them there before? There were several things that puzzled him for which he could find no answers.

15

Upon his return Kyle went in search of Shad whom he found sitting on a rock with his tail in the water, and took it upon himself to confound him with a question or two that he reckoned needed answering.

'It's said that the island just popped out from the sea one day,' he reasoned. 'It sounds strange but Morgan says it happens sometimes. Is that how you think it came here?'

'Yes, I've heard it said that the fire mountain came from *under* the sea. It must have been sleeping there, lying in wait,' Shad announced solemnly.

Carys had sidled up followed by Morgan, and gave a shudder at his words. 'How horrid,' she exclaimed.

'Oh no,' Shad replied, shaking his head. 'You must think of it as a doorway to another time and world.'

'Well, put like that ... ' Morgan began. Then

she stopped herself. 'In other words, it's certainly not a safe place to stay.'

Kyle ignored this last remark and continued with what he had in mind. 'We have to return to the cave to search for the pearl, and as I would find it impossible to retrace my steps, I will have to rely on Finn. I would never have been able to discover its whereabouts on my own. But why did Finn not take us there in the first place, if he knew the way?'

Shad grinned. 'Because he didn't ... know the way, I mean. He just followed the path the pirates took. He will remember it now - from high above - while *you* on the ground will not. Gulls have much better vision than us and can even see colours invisible to our eyes.'

'That's all very well,' Kyle agreed, 'but it still doesn't explain how I seemed to go on and on and yet get nowhere. I almost felt that if I were to turn round and go backwards I would most likely come face to face with wherever I wanted to be.'

'Like *Alice* in *Through the Looking Glass*,' Carys giggled, listening to the last bit of the conversation.

But Shad had no intention of getting side-tracked. 'Having set foot here, you cannot expect things to follow the same pattern as that from where you came,' he continued patiently. 'Didn't you name the island *Other World?* And so it is.'

This didn't explain things to Kyle's liking, but before he could go further into the matter there came a sudden exclamation from Carys, whose thoughts had reverted to the pirates and how they had slipped away without any reprisals.

'Tomb robbers! That's what they are!' she frowned. 'We shouldn't be letting them get away with it. What can we do?'

'Nothing,' Kyle replied glumly. 'It's the sort of thing pirates do.'

'Oh yes, we *can* do something,' Morgan declared vehemently. 'And I'll show you.'

She hurried back to the tent she shared with Carys and came back with something in her hand. It was the length of cord given to her as a gift from Marilla, the Weather Witch.

'Here,' she held it out to Shad. 'Follow their ship. Untie the third knot and hide it somewhere on board.'

Kyle and Carys looked at Morgan approvingly.

'Wow,' Kyle enthused, 'what a brilliant idea. I would never have thought of that.'

'Nor me,' Carys breathed. 'Will you do it, Shad?'

'Of course,' he replied at once. 'They know the legend – anyone who steals the king's crown is cursed. I will go quickly to see that the deed is done before they sail too far.'

With which he turned and dived into the sea.

......

During that very night far out on the ocean the pirate ship rode on furiously before the wind, the sails flapping wildly, cracking, and then snapping like a thunderclap. It was spun over the waves and tossed into a howling gale as the storm set in. When the wind died down at last, there was no trace of the ship.

16

With Finn as guide, the three of them set off to familiarize themselves with the cave. And this time, either due to the animated conversation that ensued or simply because his attention was not so focused, it seemed to Kyle that the journey there took less than half the time it did before. But things didn't always make sense; they appeared to get a little mixed up.

It was the same with the inside of the cave. The floor gleamed with flowstones that should have taken millions of years to form from ancient sea creatures, and yet it was not that old. The limestone walls glistening with water droplets would also have evolved over time. And the same was true of the small stalactites that hung from the roof, appearing like tiny lanterns in the half light.

It was all most intriguing. They looked round hopefully for Finn but could see no sign of him.

However they moved forward with caution, aware that somewhere in its depths resided a monster of some considerable size. But they heard it before they saw it: a sound like a loud snuffling and snoring drifted across to them.

'It sounds like it's asleep wherever it is,' Carys said, forgetting to whisper, her voice causing strange echoes that bounced off the roof and walls.

'Sssh, you'll wake it up,' Kyle hissed urgently.

But the warning came too late.

A loud roar filled the space they were in, causing Carys to catch hold of Morgan's sleeve as she gave a little scream of fright. Morgan took hold of her protectively whilst she and Kyle peered fearfully in every direction.

It was then that they caught their first glimpse of the creature as it began to uncoil from a ledge where it lay hidden, lifting its head to stare at them with hypnotic yellow eyes. It resembled something between a huge lizard and a sea serpent. As they watched transfixed, they saw that its long body and tail were studded all over with tough armour plated scales.

Rising up in obvious annoyance at being disturbed, it adopted a menacing pose, swinging its upper body from side to side, as if sizing them up. Then it began to move slowly forward. Its claws scraped over the stony floor, its scales causing a slithering, scratching sound as they slid over one another. Within its gaping mouth its sharp, serrated teeth were clearly visible.

Where was Finn? Wasn't that his shadow at the entrance of the cave?

There was a sudden whirr of wings and the familiar great backed gull swooped towards them uttering a deep trumpeting call. It had the immediate effect of startling the dragon which backed away in alarm.

But Finn did not attack the creature. Instead he dropped something from his webbed feet that landed beside them on the stone floor.

Morgan picked it up with a cry. *It was his reed pipe.* And she knew immediately what was expected of her. Placing it to her lips, she blew gently upon it, turning towards the dragon at the same time.

First of all it thrashed out with its tail and swung round to snap at her ferociously. But in another moment it had given a huge yawn, curled itself round in a circle and tucked its head under its tail. Then it began to snore.

Morgan could hardly believe it. How clever of Finn to have thought of such a simple solution. And now since the dragon was asleep it gave them time to look for the coveted pearl.

But where to start looking?

'Maybe there's a pool somewhere close,' Kyle suggested. 'Oysters like water.'

'Yes, in deep water caves. But this isn't one,' Morgan argued, 'and only special oysters have pearls. What we're searching for is a special pearl, one that most likely belonged to the dead king – part of his treasure - maybe even from his crown which the pirates stole.'

'Yes but …' Carys shook her head. 'Think … if the dragon sometimes carries the pearl around in its teeth, as legend tells, it could be hidden somewhere on its body.'

'That's a thought,' Morgan nodded. 'Let's have a look while we have the chance.'

They approached the sleeping dragon with caution, very timidly, just in case he slept with one eye open. But he neither moved nor stirred in his slumber, only giving loud snores now and then.

Kyle lifted each of the creature's small ear flaps which resembled that of a sea lion, and felt around for any small object hidden behind its scales.

He was very disappointed at finding nothing there. Carys looked between its claws, and they even peeped beneath its tail, which proved quite dangerous since it occasionally lashed it around in its sleep.

They peered under all the rocks and ledges they could find, lifting up fronds of seaweed to find where small crabs and shellfish hid - all to no avail.

At last they had to admit defeat for the time being. It was all so disheartening, but if the pearl existed it must be *somewhere.*

'We shall have to get back and ask around a bit more. Someone must know something we don't.' Morgan reasoned. 'What do you say, Carys?'

'I think the same,' she nodded. 'But I have this feeling that I get sometimes – call it a sixth sense. We're going to get lucky in a strange way.'

'Well, hope you're right. Let's go,' Kyle muttered, glancing back at the still sleeping dragon. 'Don't forget Finn's pipe. I've a feeling we're going to need it again sooner than we think.'

Carys was right about her sixth sense. She predicted that something would happen soon, and it did.

Kyle was walking along the beach the next day, when he heard someone shouting. He couldn't think where the sound had come from until he happened to look skywards. He wasn't prepared for what he saw.

A fair distance above him sailed a blue balloon attached to a basket. Leaning over the side was a man waving and yelling at the top of his voice.

'Ha-loo … ha-loo there! How yer doin'?'

Kyle waved back and then hurried off to find the girls. They were as surprised as him.

Whoever could it be up there? And where did

he come from?

They were questions that would have remained unanswered had it not been that the individual decided to land right there on the beach. Down he came in his basket with hardly a bump, making a smooth landing on the soft sand.

He was a strange character wearing a small bushy moustache; a clay pipe hung from one lip which he chewed on continuously. His face was creased into a permanently wide smile, a feature perfectly suited to the little pork pie hat perched precariously on one side of his head.

It was impossible not to like him.

'Me name's Paddy O'Rourk, so it is,' he exclaimed with an infectious grin. 'Oi've bin on a visit, so I 'ave.'

'Really?' Morgan looked surprised. 'I can't believe there's anyone round here to visit.'

'Oh, but there is, indeed; there's me friend, Marilla, the Weather Witch. You'll be knowing 'er now, for sure.'

'Well, yes, we certainly know her,' Carys replied.

Paddy nodded. 'She asked for me to keep an eye open for ye'.

'Really?' Morgan said again. 'But why?'

'She wanted to say *well done*.'

'Well done for what?'

'Why, for the way ye handled those pirates. Reckon you sent a good wind after 'em.'

'Oh,' Morgan looked uncomfortable, but Carys pressed her hand.

'It was well done, that it was,' Paddy nodded. 'She be a friend o' mine, old Marilla. I bin 'aving rope winds from 'er for years.'

'They're magic winds,' Kyle mused. 'Wish we could take some of those back with us when we go out fishing with our crew back home. We'd be forever in their good books.'

'That's something I hadn't thought of,' Morgan grinned.

'I bought several of 'em,' Paddy went on. 'They be ri't useful to I.'

'I can imagine,' Kyle chuckled. 'You must need lots of wind for what you do.'

'Want to join me?' Paddy asked, pointing to his balloon.

'Wow! Yes – I'd like to give it a go. But we wouldn't all fit into your basket, would we?' Kyle exclaimed. 'What about you two?' He looked expectantly at the girls.

They looked at each-other and nodded.

'Oi'll take two of ye; any two at a time,' Paddy declared.

So it was that Morgan and Carys volunteered to go first, rather to Kyle's surprise. But as Morgan was the eldest she was usually the one who led, and it was generally Kyle who stood aside.

In next to no time they had both scrambled aboard to join Paddy, and once airborne they waved frantically and shouted to let Kyle know all was well. The balloon seemed to blend in with the sky once they reached a certain height, and Kyle had to shade his eyes against the sun in order to track them. At last they drifted out of sight and it seemed they were gone for ages as he scanned the empty skies impatiently waiting for their return.

At last he was rewarded with a speck on the horizon growing bigger as he watched. Then as the balloon came closer, he could make out the girls and Paddy quite distinctly, the girls shouting and waving as before.

Once they had made a landing it was difficult for Kyle to get a word in, such were the many garbled versions of the journey.

'We soared right over the Dragon's Teeth,' Carys reported. 'The sea was quite rough out there.'

'And we saw several small dots of islands we didn't expect,' Morgan added. 'A really exciting way to travel, tell us what you think.'

Paddy held out a supporting hand which Kyle ignored as he jumped in beside him, such was his eager haste. There was plenty of room for just the two of them inside.

'Ready?' Paddy grinned. And in no time they had lift-off and rose swiftly into the air.

Kyle leaned over the side and waved to the girls below, then gave himself up to the pure ecstasy of finding himself amongst the clouds.

'It all looks so different from up here,' he said craning his neck to see both above and below him at the same time. 'The island is so small.'

Paddy chuckled in reply. 'That there's a strange bit o' rock, so it is; but there be smaller, better ones further on – wait and see.'

The wind was kind to them, lifting and pushing them along on gentle currents of air. Kyle noticed the several strands of rope with various knots, both tied and untied, that Paddy had placed to one side.

They sailed over the Dragon's Teeth rocks, as Morgan had said, and below them Kyle spotted several tiny dots that Paddy told him were islands where lived the Seal People. He was quick to point out that he didn't mean the selkies – seals that lived in the water - but people who were hunters of seals. Once upon a time they used the skins of the seals they caught to clothe themselves in.

'So they became known as the Seal People,' Kyle exclaimed. 'I would like to meet one of them.'

Paddy smiled and nodded, while Kyle leaned over as far as he could to get another glimpse of the little islands standing high in the water, all of which seemed to change in shape and colour as he looked at them. They appeared to lie in the sky, floating with the clouds.

Then as they made their way back he told of their quest to find the sea pearl in the cave of the dragon, and explained about the feud between Finn and the Sea Witch.

Paddy whistled. 'Well isn't that the best thing oi've heard in donkey's years!'

Kyle wondered if this meant he didn't believe him, but his next words suggested otherwise.

'Oi'll tell ye what oi'll do. Ye say you want t' meet one of them seal folk; well I ain't promising, but I knows 'em. Oi'll get one o' 'em to come over and see ye. Mimh be a friend o' mine. He knows all about everyt'ng.'

So saying, he landed Kyle safely on the beach, with the promise of returning very soon.

'I'm gonna head on now,' he said, waving cheerily to them all as he lifted off from the beach. And they watched his balloon until it was just a speck on the horizon as he sailed away into the sunset.

'Well, that made for an interesting day,' Morgan concluded as they sat around a little later sharing their supper. 'I wonder what tomorrow will bring.'

'Paddy again, with his friend, I hope,' Kyle smiled. 'Strange name Mimh … must have something to do with seals. Just hope he comes up with some idea that can help us.'

18

Paddy's friend was the strangest looking little man they had ever set eyes on. It was difficult to determine his age, but he had a dog-like gentle puppy face with large mild eyes and an abundance of whiskers; very reminiscent of a seal. In fact he was reputed to be one of the oldest members of that clan still called 'the seal people.'

He had travelled across the sea with Paddy in his air balloon, and was so full of colourful news and information that for once it seemed that Paddy was scarcely able to get a word in. Someone closely associated with the people of the sea was Shad, who also joined the group as they made a circle round the little man, eager to hear what he had to say.

'Once,' Mimh said, 'we used to hunt and kill the seals and wear their skins. That's how we came to be named *the seal people*. Mayhap ye know the song:

> *I am a man upon the land*
> *I am a selkie in the sea.'*

But Morgan, Kyle and Carys had never heard the words before or known of such a song. So Mimh continued:

'Once upon a time, long ago, it was the habit of the fisher-folk to go killing seals. But on this day I speak of, there was a man who went seal hunting who called on his neighbour to go with him to the sea caves. This man's wife was away from home, so he was minding the baby and said he couldn't go with him. But they thought out a plan where it was decided to take the baby with them in their boat - one covered with animal skins - that had oars or a sail, known as a Curragh.

'The baby was wrapped up and placed in a cradle in the bow of the boat. When they arrived at the mouth the cave, the father took the cradle and put it on a ledge inside and left it there. Not long after they did this, a great storm arose and a wave almost washed them away. Fearing their exit would be cut off, they rushed for their boat, reaching it just in time.

'In so doing, they forgot all about the baby. They couldn't get back to rescue it, so had to return home without it.

'About two days later, the storm at sea stopped and the sea became calm. So the men went out again to see if they could find any trace of the baby. When they reached the cave they found a big seal nursing what they thought was a baby seal at the breast in the manner of a human mother. As they approached, the seal dropped it on the floor of the cave and rushed into the sea, leaving it behind. They went up and examined it, thinking they were going to find a baby seal, but instead they found their own baby.

'He was quite warm and unharmed, and they took him away back home to the great joy of the mother and all the neighbours. In time he grew up to be a fine young man and an amazing swimmer.'

Mimh stopped and looked around at his audience.

'How long ago was that?' Kyle asked at last.

'Why, a few hundred years ago, I do believe,'

Mimh replied. 'But from that day to this, us folk never again hunted the seals. It was for the kindness that mother seal had shown to us. And that's how we became known as 'the seal people.'

'I think it's a lovely story,' Morgan exclaimed, looking round at the others for their response.

'Well, 'tis true enough,' Mimh replied. 'And now I must tell ye what I can of another story; of the legend of those who ruled these parts.'

'Yes, please,' Carys nodded. 'We know little of that either.'

'Well, this king whose name is lost in time was out fishing one day 'tis said when he caught a mermaid in his net. They fell in love, but he couldn't live in the sea neither could she live on land. They exchanged gifts, he with his crown of gold, she with a sea pearl that she hung around his neck. But one day when out in his boat, he was caught in a storm and drowned.

'The mermaid and her friends put him in a cave, hidden at that time beneath the sea. A stone still bears his name. Within the tomb they buried his crown and left a sea dragon to guard it and the pearl. It's said the monster often carried the pearl around in its mouth. No-one knew what happened to it, but the story goes that it's still hidden somewhere close at hand.'

'The dragon couldn't carry a small pearl around in its mouth, it might swallow it,' Kyle reasoned. That must have just been part of the legend.'

'A good point; so I was wrong,' Morgan frowned. 'It was not a jewel from the king's crown after all.'

'No,' Mimh replied. 'My people have seen the sea dragon and we believe the real treasure lies with the pearl still protected within its shell which the dragon guards.'

'That makes much more sense,' Kyle agreed.

Mimh smiled broadly, showing a set of very white teeth. 'So you must look for a shell. And what does an oyster shell remind you of?'

They thought for a moment, and then Carys exclaimed 'A *scale* ... *a dragon scale.* Of course, the crown was a treasure itself, but the pearl was what the king cherished most.'

'Try looking under the dragon's scales,' Mimh advised. 'We find many small fish hide themselves under bigger fish's scales. And there's another thing: beware that on certain times at high tide the Sea Witch will enter the cave without warning.'

Then Paddy, who had been listening and nodding at intervals, suddenly came up with something he recalled that interested him.

'There was a man that I saw t' other day, building a wall to keep out the sea. And that was a foolish act, so it was,' he announced, shaking his head vigorously.

'Finn did that,' Kyle replied. 'Finn tried to keep the sea back from his bit of the shore. The thought was good - he meant well - but the Sea Witch made him pay for it dearly.'

'Ah well, some say *we* were once under a spell worked by her you call the Sea Witch,' Mimh said, rubbing his chin. 'She changed us into seals until it pleased her to turn us back to our proper shapes again. And at last we have shed our skins and grown legs once more.'

'Really?' Morgan looked at him and grinned. 'You have so many stories to tell, I'm sure I don't know which to believe.'

Mimh's answer was to give a grunt and shake his head. 'That's for you to decide. As for me, I must be on my way and Paddy with me. But don't you go forgetting what I've said. Look for a scale that's a bit different from those around it; one that stands out.'

'We won't forget, and thanks so much for all your help,' Kyle shouted after the pair as they made their way back to the air balloon waiting on the beach.

19

They rose early on the morning they decided to venture to the cave, setting out with a confidence they were far from feeling.

Jac had decided to accompany them this time, since the big gull of which he was afraid was nowhere to be seen.

The sky was a dark, heavy blue grey; ominous; foreboding. There was a storm brewing, and they couldn't help wondering if the Sea Witch was aware of their intentions.

They tried to speak softly once they had entered the cave, since the sound of their voices had a way of echoing that made them afraid the slightest sound would alert anyone of their presence. A colony of bats hung from the roof which made them nervous. Could it be that they were being watched?

Then Carys gave a gasp as she realized that in her haste she had forgotten to bring the all-important wind pipe belonging to Finn, whose sound would lull the dragon to sleep.

Quickly she went outside to speak to Jac, who obligingly put his head on one side to listen. Then she positioned her hands in the familiar way as if she were playing on Finn's pipe, moving her fingers and making musical sounds. Jac had watched her doing this before, and in response he emitted a sharp *'kraa'*.

Good. It was his turn to do something. Was the thing she wanted in her tent? That was the place she kept it.

Off he went with a whirr of his wings, his mistress's words of encouragement following him.

Back in the cave the others were sure the Sea Witch was listening to them. They could hear her creeping into crevices, tip-toeing between the rocks – whispering – chuckling - hissing; gradually losing patience as she tried to reach those places that were just out of her reach. Then suddenly she made a rush and sprang forward with a piercing shriek that caused the walls to echo with her cry. She stretched out with grasping hands, greedy to take all that came within the space her arms could encompass.

Morgan linked hands with Kyle and also Carys, who had joined them. She was remembering Mimh's warning that at certain times the Sea Witch could enter the cave without warning.

'Let's hope the water doesn't rise too high before Jac can get back,' Kyle frowned, 'otherwise he won't be able to reach us.'

Carys nodded. Then she said 'think positively. He'll be here in another few minutes. As for the water … he doesn't like that any-more than I do.'

'That's a point,' Morgan added. 'You'd better leave, Carys, before the water gets too high, since you can't swim. Even Kyle and I won't be able to stay long. We know one thing: the bats show that the water level never goes beyond a certain point, otherwise they wouldn't stay.'

But the Sea Witch wasn't the only danger they had to contend with. The sea dragon had risen from its lair and was approaching them even as she spoke.

They had forgotten how big it was, as it slowly shuffled forward awkwardly on stumpy feet, flexing its body while turning its head from side to side, thrashing its tail as it emitted a hissing spitting sound.

As it came closer, Carys suddenly took a deep breath and concentrated on the bats hanging from the roof above. She tried to remember the vision and energy her grandmother brought to a subject when she wished to exert her will.

Seconds later the bats struck at the dragon's head, swooping, twittering, dipping and darting, in one swirling mass. The sudden onslaught afforded the three of them valuable time to move quickly away from danger. But the creature coming so close almost seemed to blow them over with its breath.

Carys felt sure that if it could speak it would say *Why do you run? There is nowhere to run to.*

Kyle's reaction was to throw a small piece of rock at the creature. 'Take that, you miserable worm!' he exclaimed.

Morgan looked anxiously over her shoulder towards the entrance of the cave hoping to see Jac's familiar shape. But there was nothing.

The water was rising alarmingly fast now, creeping up to their knees, reaching towards their waist. They couldn't afford to wait much longer for help to arrive.

The bats had dispersed after a few moments, and as a result the sea dragon continued its attack of aggressive behaviour. Turning round quickly, it gave a massive and ferocious swish of its tail threatening to cut them to pieces.

But once again Carys came to their rescue by taking in a full deep breath and exhaling it in an explosive burst directed at the dragon, causing its tail to hang motionless in mid-air for a few precious seconds, giving them just enough time to escape being lashed by it.

It was a heart stopping moment. Afterwards Morgan and Kyle could only look at Carys with amazed admiration.

Then there came to their ears a familiar call, a loud *'kraa'* sound. It was Jac who flew swiftly to them dropping the precious wind pipe into Carys's outstretched hand.

She quickly placed it to her lips and began to play a few notes. At once the dragon stopped mid tracks and shook its head from side to side, as if to rid itself of the sound. But the act achieved the desired result causing it to drop to the ground, curl itself up where it lay and tuck its head under its tail, as it had done once before. Then it began to snore.

'Quick! While we have the chance! Let's look for the pearl!' Kyle urged. But Morgan thought first of Carys.

'You go back to the beach,' she instructed. 'We can manage here, but if the water rises too high you will have to swim for it, and we might not be able to help you.'

So Carys quickly left, disappointed at not being included in the exciting finish but relieved to be escaping a watery fate.

Kyle and Morgan had to work fast since the water was now rising at an alarming rate. It would make the search for the pearl that much more difficult with every moment that passed.

'The upper part of its body is the most likely place to look. That's where its great claws would reach without much effort. You search one side, I'll do the other,' Morgan advised.

'The scales look so different under the water,' Kyle replied. 'They gleam and flash like gems.'

'Look for one that's different,' Morgan urged.

They continued to search for what seemed an age as the precious seconds ticked away.

And then suddenly Kyle gave a shout. 'Here! Look here!'

Morgan bent over and stared at the scale which Kyle pointed at, one that shimmered green and gold beneath the water. It lay between two large scales beneath the dragon's neck.

'That's it, then. Can you prise it free?'

'I think so.' Kyle struggled for a moment, and then looked up with the prize in his hand. 'Now let's make sure it's the right one,' he muttered.

He then produced the penknife he always travelled with, and inserted the blade into the opening of the shell. He then gently pulled the shell open and felt around inside to find the pearl.

'Here it is,' he exclaimed, holding it up to show Morgan. They caught their breath as they became aware how large and fine it was. Once in the light, it glowed in a myriad of colours.

'*A rainbow pearl,*' Morgan gasped. 'That's amazing! It's something unheard of!'

Kyle held it in his hand for a moment, trying to imagine how it had evolved: the rarest of coincidences over many years had worked this miracle from maybe just a grain of sand.

Then he gave a sigh of relief.

'I'm just glad we found it in time. See … I'll put

it in my zip pocket where it's safe … but we'll have to leave, pronto. You ready to dive?'

Morgan nodded, and they both took deep breaths and struck the water at the same time.

……

With the pearl at last safely in their possession, all that remained - until they returned it to the Sea Witch - was to let Carys and Shad have a view of it.

Carys was delighted that she was able to see the treasure at last, but warned them not to let Jac get sight of it. 'He'd love to fly off with it,' she laughed.

They called for Shad soon after they returned, and were rewarded by the utter astonishment he displayed when examining it.

'What a pearl! Like a coloured bubble! I can't believe it!' he shouted, clapping his hands. There's white and black pearls; even pink pearls; but there has never been a rainbow pearl before. It's so beautiful but …' he stopped and shook his head, 'but what a waste to give it to the Sea Witch. It's just a pawn in a game to her.'

'Exactly what we were thinking,' Morgan nodded. 'But this might be the last test the Sea Witch has set us; that the pearl will so bewitch us with its beauty we cannot part with it, and decide to keep it after all.'

'Well, we're not going to play her little games anymore,' Kyle retorted. 'We will do what we have to, as soon as possible. That's what we came here for. If it will save Finn from a life-time's slavery to her in one form or another, then so be it.'

They all agreed heartily and looked forward to the next day, which would also be the time they must think of packing up their things. It would soon be time to leave.

20

As soon as the time had been decided, they called for Shad to be in at the last. Then Morgan told the three of them to wait and watch, as she climbed to the top of the highest rock she could find on that part of the shore. Here she stood for a moment in silence looking down at the sea shimmering below her. Then in a voice that was lifted up and carried on the wind, she cried:

'I demand Sea Witch that you renounce the curse you laid on Finn!'

And she threw the pearl of many colours far out into the sea.

At the very same instant that it touched the surface a great spout of water in the shape of a hand rose up to receive it and drew it down into the depths below. Then it was gone - and the sea grew calm as if nothing had happened.

There was a stunned silence. No-one had expected the outcome to end in such a dramatic manner. And almost before a word was spoken, there came a great rumbling from the mountain behind them accompanied by puffs of smoke. The fire mountain was waking up, and the ground beneath them began to shake.

In the confusion the episode of the pearl was almost forgotten and with their belongings already packed and waiting in the boat, there seemed no reason to delay in view of the current danger that threatened.

'We'll be making a move now then,' Kyle announced, being the first to gather his thoughts, and he held out his hand to Shad. 'Thanks for everything; we couldn't have done it without you.'

Morgan and Carys hugged him and murmured their farewells. But once they had safely pushed off from the shore, Shad climbed aboard and pressed something into Morgan's hand. It was a thin rope with just two knots tied in it.

'I had it from Finn – last time I saw him,' he said. 'It's from Marilla. She wishes you a fair wind to get you home. Goodbye.'

And with that, he slipped into the sea and was gone.

Morgan untied the first knot and the wind came to her call, blowing with a fresh breeze, pushing them before it.

At the tiller Kyle found the boat quickened to his touch; below the hull, the water sang as they passed. But as they steered clear of the island, they could see the mountain puffing out even more smoke, rumbling and roaring louder than before.

Then Morgan untied the second knot. Once again the wind came to her call, and the boat skimmed over the waves like a flying fish. Kyle hardly touched the tiller. He shouted, but the wind drowned his voice, while Carys held on with rising excitement as she climbed and fell with the waves imagining herself to be a bird, swaying to the roll of the boat. She had found her sea legs at last.

Suddenly a noise like thunder rent the air; the island appeared to rock from side to side as great waves broke over it, rather like a capsized ship at the mercy of the current.

'The mountain's going to blow its top!' Kyle exclaimed, pointing.

And looking back they saw the volcano suddenly become a fire fountain, both beautiful and dramatic, as it hurled showers of red embers into the air.

'What will happen to the dragon?' Carys gasped.

'The cave will be blocked, but the dragon is a sea dragon so it will just slip away beneath the waves,' Morgan replied.

And as she spoke, a curtain of mist rose up and covered everything. There was no sign of the island. It was gone – swallowed up by the ocean.

'What an ending to the story,' Carys continued in a more sober tone.

'Well it isn't over – yet,' Kyle pointed out. 'We still have to meet up with Finn.'

Morgan gave a sigh of contentment. 'I wonder when that will be. Soon, I hope.'

'We've been away so long, the others will wonder where we've got to,' Carys grinned.

'I hope they didn't put out boats to go looking for us; that's what would happen back in our fishing village,' Morgan frowned.

'Oh, no,' Carys reassured her. 'They'll be much

too busy getting on with their own lives to bother about us.'

'Mm, hope you're right,' Kyle chuckled. 'Anyway, we'll soon find out.'

21

It was strange yet somehow comforting to be back again in familiar surroundings.

The old camper belonging to Cary's travelling companions was still parked on its usual site, and coming upon it suddenly from the seaward side tucked away among the cliffs was most reassuring.

Jac, especially, made it clear how glad he was to be back in familiar territory and showed his appreciation by hopping from one shoulder to another, emitting loud squawks, which made them all laugh.

As regard to her friends, as Carys predicted they were received with a certain reserve, although this was offset by a considerable amount of good humour.

'We thought Carys might have made you disappear in a puff of smoke,' Ben chuckled.

'You've realized she practises magic now and then,' he grinned, turning to the others.

'We've had a taste of it,' Kyle replied. 'And as it happened, it came in rather useful.'

'You were just lucky then,' was the teasing response. They all laughed, but Morgan preferred to add her own comments.

'Her grandmother's 'spells' - as she likes to put it - saved us from catastrophes on several occasions,' she added in her friend's defence.

This was greeted with some surprise.

'You must tell us about that; we'd like to hear the details,' Josh replied, giving Carys a sideways wink she pretended to ignore.

'Jac played his part too,' Morgan added. 'We couldn't have managed without him.'

'Sounds like you had more of an exciting time then you like to admit,' Izzy giggled. 'Maybe Jac will let us into some of his secrets sometime.'

After the usual banter had been exchanged on both sides, the party settled down and swapped bits of news - Morgan, Kyle and Carys being careful not to divulge too much of their adventures - merely saying that they had landed on a part of the coast affording little of interest, but where they had spent an enjoyable time camping, fishing, and sunbathing.

Morgan and Kyle then made clear their intention of setting up camp and staying a little longer before returning home.

The day after they arrived, and for several days after, they searched for any sign of Finn. But there was no trace, not even a significantly large gull which drew their attention. The beach was deserted except for a few people bathing or those who came to admire the view.

And then about a week later when they had almost given up hope, they had a surprise.

As Morgan and Kyle sat looking out to sea, with Carys doing a spot of sunbathing, they heard a shout coming from further along the beach. A figure was waving to them.

The three held their breath. *It was Finn* – the *very same Finn they had grown to know and love years ago.* As he came closer they could see he seemed not to have changed a bit, with his tangled red hair, green eyes, and familiar grin.

He held out his arms to them and smiled - his warm mysterious smile - just as they remembered.

'I'm here because of you,' he said softly, obviously not trusting himself to say more. He just stood and looked at them, while they stared back, too lost for words, hardly daring to breathe or take their eyes off him for fear he was merely an illusion and might disappear at any moment.

In relating the story, there is little more to add. Morgan being closer to him than her brother or Carys would always keep his words in her heart:

Wherever we go from here, it will be a new adventure. Just remember that even if at times I seem a bit out of touch I will always come back to you.

And so it happened that what she thought was the end, was only the beginning.

....